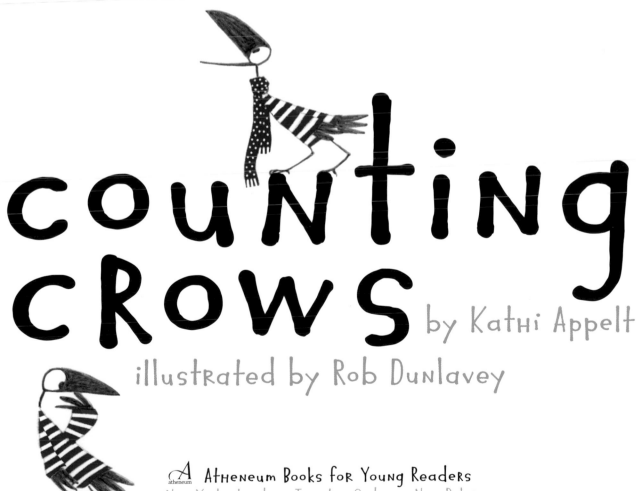

COUNTING CROWS

by Kathi Appelt

illustrated by Rob Dunlavey

A Atheneum Books for Young Readers
atheneum
New York   London   Toronto   Sydney   New Delhi

ATHENEUM BOOKS FOR YOUNG READERS

An imprint of Simon & Schuster Children's Publishing Division
1230 Avenue of the Americas, New York, New York 10020
Text copyright © 2015 by Kathi Appelt
Illustrations copyright © 2015 by Rob Dunlavey

For information about special discounts for bulk purchases, please contact
Simon & Schuster Special Sales at 1-866-506-1949
or business@simonandschuster.com.
The Simon & Schuster Speakers Bureau can bring authors to your live event. For more
information or to book an event,
contact the Simon & Schuster Speakers Bureau at 1-866-248-3049 or visit our website
at www.simonspeakers.com.
Book design by Debra Sfetsios-Conover
The text for this book is set in Pocket.
The illustrations for this book are rendered in pencil and digital color.
Manufactured in China
1214 SCP
First Edition
2 4 6 8 10 9 7 5 3 1
Library of Congress Cataloging-in-Publication Data
Appelt, Kathi, 1954-
Counting crows / Kathi Appelt ; illustrated by Rob Dunlavey. — First edition.
p. cm
Summary: The reader is invited to count hungry crows as they hunt for savory snacks.
ISBN 978-1-4424-2327-5 (hardcover) — ISBN 978-1-4424-8332-3 (eBook)
[1. Stories in rhyme. 2. Crows—Fiction. 3. Counting.] I. Dunlavey, Rob, illustrator. II. Title.
PZ8.3.A554Cm 2015
[E]—dc23
2014002094

To Kimbo, for wings and pies, with love—K. A.

For Stephanie—R. D.

One, two, three

crows in a tree.

THREE roly-poly bugs,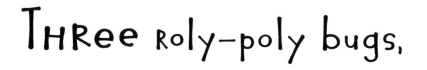

THRee Ripe mangoes.

THREE FOR THE counting crows.

THREE, by jango!

One,

two,

three,

four,

five,

six

crows in a nest
of straw and sticks.

Six salty peanuts,

six ripe plums.

Six for the counting crows.

Yum, yum, **yum!**

One,

two,

THREE,

four,

five,

six,

seven,

eight,

nine

crows on a line.

Nine little spicy ants,

NiNe RouNd cRackeRs.
NiNe foR the counting cRows.

NiNe, by smackeRs!

One, two, three
crows in a tree.

Four, five, six
crows in the sticks.

Seven, eight, nine

crows on a line.

Ten in a row,

ten crows CROW!

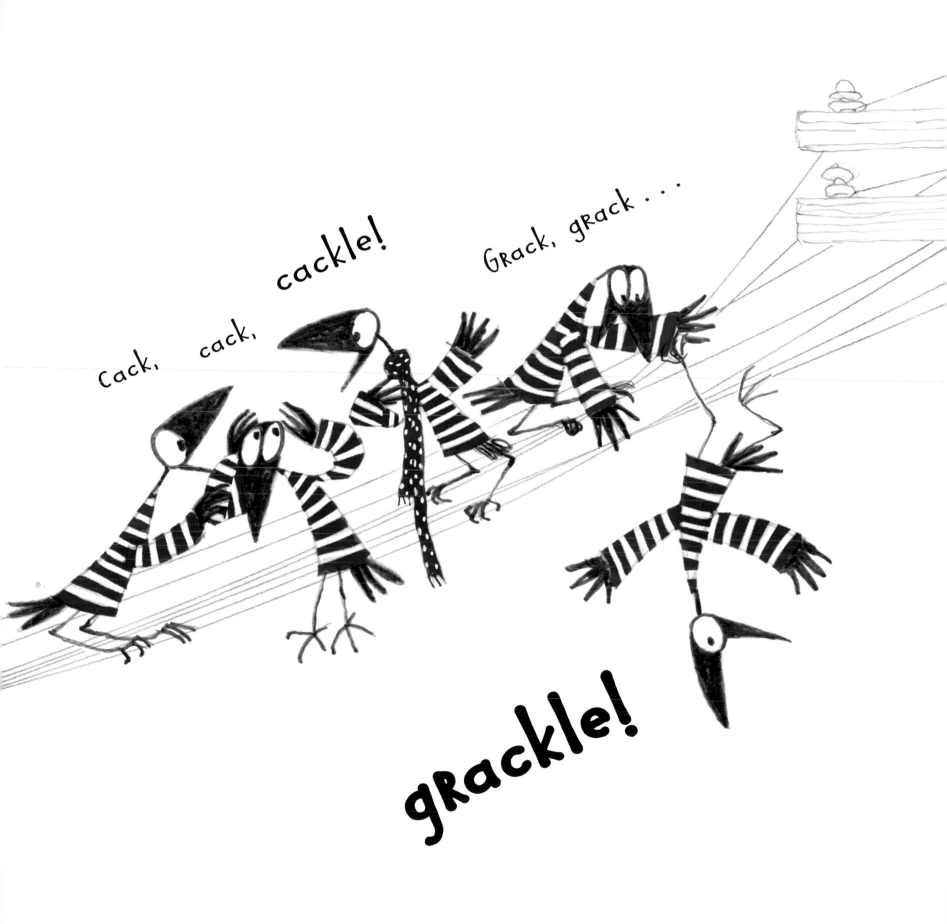

Ten crunchy crickets,

ten green peppers.

Ten for the counting crows.

Yep, yep, **yeppers!**

One, two, three, four,

five, six, seven . . .

eight . . .

nine . . .

ten . . .

eleven!

Eleven bright berries,

eleven sweet peas.

Eleven for the counting crows.

Eleven, if you please!

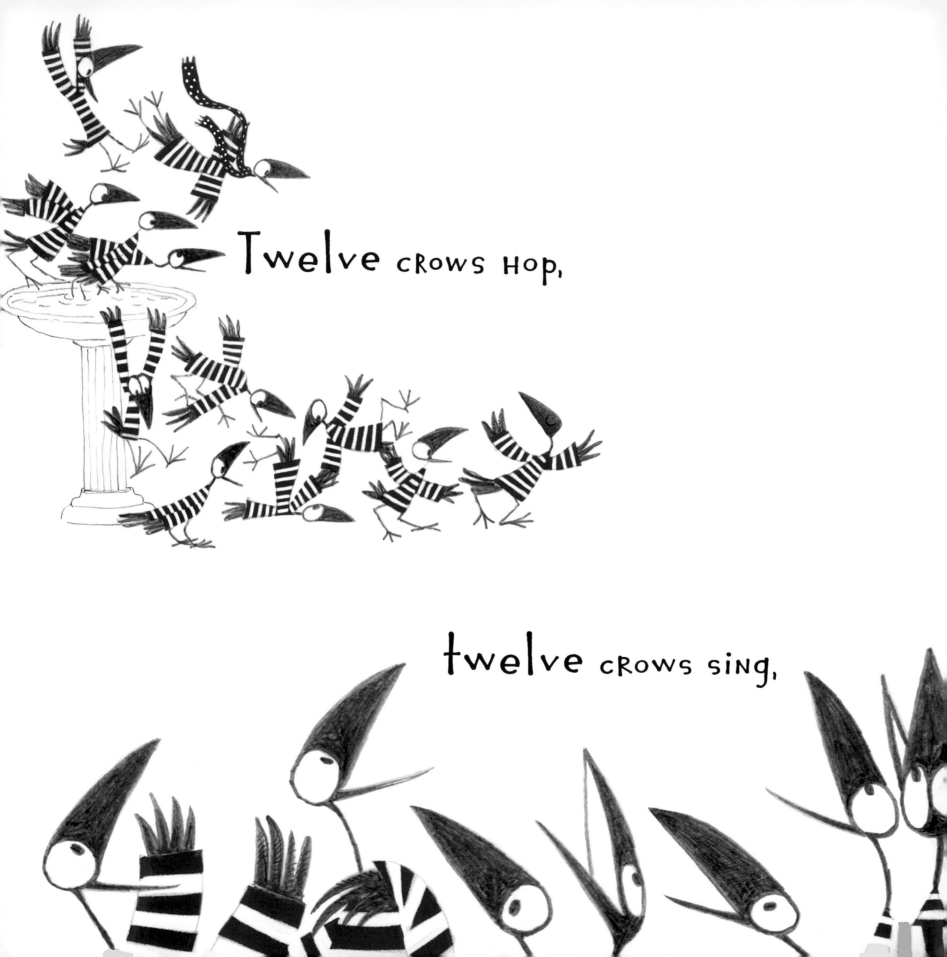

Twelve CROWS HOP,

twelve CROWS SING,

twelve on a park bench,
wing by **wing.**

Twelve chewy chips,

twelve slimy snails . . .

One CAT counts

twelve crows' twelve tails!

One, two, three,

see ya, **tree.**

five,

FouR,

six,

aloHa, sticks.

eleven,

twelve . . .

Ten,

Twelve crows flap,

twelve crows fly . . .

one dozen counting crows . . .